Bonnie Blair

Power on Ice

Bonnie Blair
Power on Ice

by Wendy Daly

A Bullseye Biography

Random House 🏠 **New York**

Photo credits: AP/Wide World Photos, pages 41, 45, 46, 51, 71, 72, 73, 74, 76, 80, 81, 83, 84, 87, 90; The Bettmann Archive, page 36; UPI/Bettmann, page 38; Blair, pages 6, 14, 17, 18, 19, 22, 27, 28, 31, 33, 50 (top), 50 (bottom), 54, 56, 63, 68.

A BULLSEYE BOOK PUBLISHED BY RANDOM HOUSE, INC.

Daly, Wendy.
Bonnie Blair : power on ice / by Wendy Daly.
p. cm. — (A bullseye biography)
Summary: Narrates the skating career of the American woman who is an Olympic gold medalist for speed skating, who came from a family of skaters, and who has skated since the age of two.
ISBN 0-679-86997-2 (pbk.)
1. Blair, Bonnie, 1964– —Juvenile literature. 2. Skaters—United States—Biography—Juvenile literature. 3. Speed skating—Juvenile literature. [1. Blair, Bonnie, 1964– . 2. Ice skaters. 3. Women—Biography. 4. Speed skating.] I. Title. II. Series.
GV850.B63D35 1996
796.332'092—dc20
[B] 95-23217

Manufactured in the United States of America 10 9 8 7 6 5 4 3 2 1

Contents

*Bonnie practicing just before the
Calgary Winter Olympics.*

1

Bonnie the Blur

Bonnie Blair is too nervous to eat. But she makes herself finish her peanut butter and jelly sandwich. It's her favorite meal before a race.

Today, Bonnie needs all the energy she can get. She hopes, in just a few hours, to become the fastest speed skater in the world. It is Monday, February 22, 1988, at the Winter Olympics in Calgary, Canada.

Now that Bonnie's plate is empty, she leaves the cafeteria. She returns to her room in the Olympic Village. She tries to relax before her big race. But it is impossible.

Bonnie is twenty-three years old. She has been skating since she was two. This afternoon she has a chance to fulfill a lifetime dream. She has a chance to win an Olympic gold medal in speed skating.

Finally, it is time to get ready. Bonnie pulls on her tight speed-skating skin, with its gray and orange design. She tucks her brown hair under her close-fitting hood.

That's it for Bonnie's outfit. No sequins. No feathers. No frills. Those are for the figure skaters. Speed skaters want nothing to get in their way.

Bonnie's main rival skates first. Christa Rothenburger is a tall, strong skater from East Germany. It takes Christa just 39.12 seconds to skate 500 meters. Christa is so fast she sets a new world record.

How can Bonnie top that? How can she beat a world record? There is only one way. Bonnie will have to set a new world record of her own. She will have to skate faster than she ever has in her life, under more pressure than she has ever faced.

Bonnie crouches down at the starting line. She digs in her left skating blade. Bonnie is relatively small for a speed skater, at 5'4½" and 125 pounds. But years of training have given her incredible strength in her legs and back.

The starting pistol cracks. Bonnie bursts onto the track with a few short, quick, powerful strokes. Then she eases into a gliding position. Her arms and legs now move in perfect rhythm.

A huge roar thunders from the grandstands. It is the applause from Bonnie's mother and father, along with her brothers, sisters, nephews, nieces, and friends. They've been cheering for Bonnie all her life. But today, all Bonnie can hear is a voice inside her, telling her she can win.

Bonnie speeds off the last turn. She is now racing down the backstretch, whizzing by the crowds at almost thirty-five miles an hour. No wonder people call her "Bonnie the Blur!"

Bonnie practically jumps across the finish line. She knows she has done her best. But she isn't sure she has won until she looks up at the electronic board.

For the second time that night, the board flashes "World Record." Bonnie has skated 500 meters in 39.10 seconds. She has beaten Christa Rothenburger's record by just two hundredths of a second! That's less time than it takes to blink your eye.

Bonnie is so excited she punches the air with her fists. Tears of joy stream down her face as she looks up toward her family. They have always believed in her. So have her supporters back home in Champaign, Illinois. She hasn't let them down.

Bonnie steps up to the Olympic victory stand. This is the happiest day of her life. The tears keep flowing. Bonnie manages a smile and sings the national anthem. The United States has a new hero.

Later, Bonnie turns to a reporter. "I feel like I'm living a dream," she says. "And I'm not sure I want it to end."

Bonnie's Olympic dreams did not end in Calgary. She went on to win a total of five gold medals. That's a record. No other American woman has ever won five Olympic gold medals in any sport.

How did she do it? How did this small, brown-haired youngster from Champaign, Illinois, become the Olympic Golden Girl?

Here is her story.

2

Born to Skate

Bonnie Blair's speed-skating career began the day she was born. Not many athletes can say that. But in Bonnie's case, there was never any doubt that she would be a skater. The proof lies in the story of her birth.

The drama began March 18, 1964, in Cornwall, New York. Bonnie's mother, Eleanor Blair, needed to go to the hospital. She was about to have a baby. That baby would turn out to be Bonnie, the sixth and last child of Eleanor and Charles Blair.

But there was one slight problem. Some of Mr. and Mrs. Blair's older children were supposed to skate in a race that afternoon. And Mr. Blair had promised to help time the skaters.

What should Mr. Blair do? Should he go with his wife to the hospital? Or should he go with his children to the ice-skating rink?

Charlie and Eleanor Blair both loved speed skating. Four of their five children were already racers. The family was devoted to the sport. The Blairs decided Charlie shouldn't miss the race.

Charlie Blair dropped his pregnant wife off at the hospital and sped to the skating rink. As the skaters raced, Eleanor Blair gave birth to baby Bonnie.

The happy news was announced over the loudspeaker at the skating rink. "Another speed skater has been born to the Blair family," the announcer said.

That's how Charlie Blair found out he had a new daughter named Bonnie. The skating rink announcer predicted that Bonnie would grow up to be a speed skater. But that day, no one could know just how fast she would be!

Bonnie at age three, already up on skates.

Bonnie's family couldn't wait to get her on the ice. Her oldest brother, Chuck, was the only non-racer in the family. He was already twenty-one years old when Bonnie was born.

Bonnie's other brother and her three sisters practically lived on the ice during the speed-skating season. There was eighteen-

14

year-old Mary, fifteen-year-old Suzy, nine-year-old Rob, and seven-year-old Angela. They started searching for a pair of skates for Bonnie as soon as she could walk.

Not too many skates are designed to fit two-year-olds. But that didn't stop the Blair family. They simply took the smallest pair of old skates that they could find. And they pulled them on, right over Bonnie's walking shoes!

Their plan worked. Wearing skates over shoes was awkward. But with only a push, Bonnie took off on the ice. Skating came to her as naturally as walking.

Just as Bonnie was learning to skate, her family moved to Champaign, Illinois. It was the perfect place to raise a family of speed skaters. Skating on frozen ponds made the cold, gray winters fun. And there were many indoor rinks that were open all year long.

Mr. Blair's job as a civil engineer kept him

busy. But he always found the time to help his kids skate. Mr. and Mrs. Blair liked the children to enter races. Bonnie entered her first race when she was just four years old!

With so many children, and so many races, the Blair family spent most of their winters at the skating rink. Little Bonnie often took her naps at the rink, in between races.

At the height of the racing season, the Blair family would pile into the car almost every weekend. They traveled to different meets around Illinois, Missouri, and Indiana. As Bonnie watched (or sometimes slept), her older sisters and brother won many races. Before long, Rob, Mary, and Suzy Blair were all national champions.

Being the baby of the family wasn't always easy for Bonnie. She was so much younger than her brothers and sisters that

Bonnie and her brother Rob and sister Angela are off to a skating meet in December 1970. Mrs. Blair hands Bonnie their bagged lunch.

they often seemed more like parents than playmates.

"It's not like I had brothers and sisters to play Monopoly with," Bonnie remembers. "I was a tagalong."

But Bonnie never caused trouble for her family. She did what she was told. She went wherever they went. Bonnie knew her parents

Bonnie's cheerful nature could be seen as early as age six. Here she wears a helmet, as she is about to skate indoors and must protect her head in case she hits the sides of the rink.

*Six-year-old Bonnie, already seriously practicing
her skating technique.*

had spent a lot of time and energy raising
their five older children. She wanted to make
life easy for them.

Bonnie's cheerful nature and her desire to
win helped to make her a great young athlete. By the age of seven, she was racing in

the Illinois State Championships.

Soon, Bonnie was no longer just the tag-along. She was a winner. *She* was the member of the Blair family people came to watch.

3

Leader of the Pack

Bonnie was a tough skater in her early days. She had to be. That's because she started out as a pack-style racer. Pack racing is like a crowded track meet...on ice!

Pack racers can't be shy. They don't race against the clock the way Olympic-style racers do. Pack skaters race against each other. They have to elbow their way to the front of the pack if they want to win the race.

"In a pack-style race," Bonnie once explained, "you get off quickly—or you don't get off."

Bonnie learned many lessons as a pack racer. Getting off to a fast start was one of them. With practice, Bonnie perfected what

Bonnie leads the pack in a 1974 Illinois State Championship.

one reporter later called her "turbo-charged start."

Bonnie also learned not to worry about being short. In pack races, she was often dwarfed by the taller speed skaters. But she didn't let that discourage her. Instead, she figured out a way to squeeze right by the bigger skaters, straight toward the finish line. What Bonnie lacked in height, she made up for in style and speed.

Bonnie brought home many trophies as a pack-style racer. She was only ten years old when she won her first National Indoor Speed Skating title. Winning this title meant that, for her age, she was one of the fastest skaters in the country.

Bonnie could have bragged about her skating. But she didn't. That's why she's remembered as a normal, fun-loving girl at Westview Elementary School in Champaign.

Her days in elementary school may sound quite normal. Bonnie earned mostly A's and B's. She loved recess. She played on a girls' softball team. And she went to a lot of slumber parties.

There was only one thing different about Bonnie, remembers one of her fifth-grade classmates. After those all-night slumber parties, "everyone else went home to crash. But Bonnie went off to skate."

Bonnie knew she loved skating right from the beginning. She knew she was happiest when she was on the ice. But she hadn't even dreamed of making it to the Olympics.

Bonnie's father was the first to even talk about the possibility. Once, when Bonnie was visiting his office, he started talking to someone about her talents. "She's going to skate in the Olympics," Mr. Blair said confidently, "and she's going to win a gold medal."

Bonnie was just twelve years old at the time. She didn't believe her father at first. But the more she thought about it, the more she liked the idea. Maybe her father was right. Maybe she could become an Olympic speed skater.

"It was *his* dream at first," Bonnie has said. "It just took a little while to make it *my* dream."

4

Setting Goals

Bonnie started working harder on her speed skating. When she was fifteen, her Olympic dreams received another boost. A Canadian speed skater who had already been in the Olympics spotted Bonnie in a crowd of pack racers.

Cathy Priestner had won a silver medal in the 1976 Winter Olympics. She studied Bonnie on the ice. She was sure that Bonnie could be a winner, too.

Bonnie's mother says that Cathy Priestner came along just at the right time. "Bonnie was at that stage when she was falling down," Mrs. Blair remembers. "She was going through a clumsy stage, but Cathy could see great potential in Bonnie and gave her a lot of encouragement."

Cathy convinced Bonnie she was ready to switch from pack racing to Olympic-style racing. No more hordes of skaters! Now Bonnie would race only in pairs. And she would race against the clock, not against the other skaters on the ice.

Bonnie made the switch quickly and easily. In 1981, when she was seventeen, she won her first national title in Olympic-style racing. The time had come for her to start training for the 1984 Olympics.

Bonnie works out on a slideboard in her family's garage in Illinois.

Bonnie lifting weights.

Bonnie began working out at Centennial High School in Champaign. She lifted weights. She cycled. She ran.

Bonnie pushed herself harder and harder. Instead of just running around the track, she ran carrying an inner tube. The inner tube was filled with sand. It weighed at least thirty pounds!

Bonnie was often the only girl in the weight room. But working out with the boys' football team never bothered her. Coach Gary Hembrough remembers driving to school in the evenings to open the weight room for his football players. When he'd arrive at 6:30, Bonnie would already be there, waiting to get in.

There was just one problem. Bonnie spent so much time training and racing she had little time for anything else. Something had to give. That something turned out to be cheerleading.

Bonnie had always loved cheerleading. She loved the movements, the crowds, the excitement. But she found it hard to be at every game. She was out of town too often at speed-skating meets.

Bonnie decided to give up cheerleading in her junior year. "I miss the cheerleading, but skating is very important to me," she told a reporter that year. "It's always been the main thing in my life. I've had to give up a lot of other things, but so far, it's been worth it."

One thing Bonnie never gave up was her schoolwork. It would have been easy for her to fall behind. But her parents made sure that didn't happen.

Mr. and Mrs. Blair wanted Bonnie to get the most out of her education. They refused to let her compete on the world circuit until she was older. International competitions would have meant too much time away from high school.

Of course, the Blairs did allow Bonnie to compete on a national level. But whenever Bonnie left town for a skating meet, her mother picked up the homework assignments and tests that Bonnie was missing. Even if it meant studying in hotel rooms, cars, and ice skating rinks, Bonnie always finished her schoolwork.

Once she finished high school, Bonnie began competing on an international level. Here she skates—and wins the World Championship—at the 1983 Indoor World Championships in Chamonix, France.

Bonnie worked out a balance between speed skating and school. But soon, her dream of competing in the Olympics created another challenge. This time, the problem was money.

Bonnie's parents were not wealthy. It was difficult to pay all the costs of Bonnie's training. Coaches cost money, and there were fees for rink time. Then there was the cost of all those out-of-town meets. Hotels. Food. Airfare. The Blairs needed help.

Bonnie came up with a plan. She decided to ask businesses in and around Champaign for donations. It would take courage to talk to local businessmen. After all, Bonnie was only seventeen years old. But she was determined to raise money for her Olympic training.

Bonnie's determination soon turned to discouragement. Everyone in the business community wished her well. But no one gave her money.

What now? A friend suggested that Bonnie call the Champaign police. It was not your ordinary call for help. But Bonnie was no ordinary girl.

The Champaign police raised more than $10,000 for Bonnie's training and travel expenses. Bonnie poses with two members of the police department.

Bonnie met Police Sergeant Jerry Schweighart at the Red Wheel Restaurant in Champaign. She showed the sergeant a piece of paper listing her expenses. She figured that she needed $7,500.

Sergeant Schweighart was impressed by Bonnie's enthusiasm and dedication. He, too, wished her well. But that wasn't the end of their meeting. Sergeant Schweighart made a promise to Bonnie. He told her that his department would raise the money she needed.

The sergeant and his fellow officers kept their word. They held bake sales and garage sales. They sold candy bars and raffle tickets. The police even started selling bumper stickers, calling Bonnie their "Favorite Speeder."

The Champaign police raised more than $10,000 for Bonnie's training and travel expenses. Soon, Champaign's "favorite speeder" was headed toward Sarajevo, Yugoslavia, the site of the 1984 Winter Olympics.

5

A Place in History

As Bonnie headed to her first Olympics, she had many things to prove. She had to show the world she could skate under pressure. She had to represent the United States proudly in a foreign country.

Luckily, there was one thing Bonnie did not have to prove at the Olympics. She did not have to prove that women could be good speed skaters. By the time the 1984 Olympics took place, women's speed skating was an accepted sport. But it hadn't always been so.

The Olympics started out as an event for men only. The ancient Greeks held the first known Olympic games in 776 B.C. Women were not allowed to compete in the sports. In

*Once all-steel skates were produced in 1850,
skating became a sport. In this 1877 lithograph,
men and women enjoy themselves on the ice
in New York City's Central Park.*

fact, women weren't even allowed into the stadium to watch the games.

Skating did not start out as an Olympic sport. In the beginning, skating was simply a form of transportation. Long before the days of cars or airplanes, skating was one of the best ways to get around quickly during the winter. Even today, skating is the fastest means of travel without the help of machines or gravity.

With today's high-tech skates, speed skaters can travel as fast as thirty-five miles an hour. But that wasn't always possible. More than 2,000 years ago, skates were made out of sharpened animal bones. Later models were made of wood and iron. As you can imagine, these primitive skates were heavy and awkward.

Finally, in 1850, a Philadelphia man named E. W. Bushnell produced the first all-steel skates. These new skates were lightweight but very strong. Now skating could be fun.

Skating clubs opened up all across the United States. The American Skating Congress held its first races in 1868. But the skating world still wasn't ready for someone like Bonnie Blair. That's because speed skating

*The first American Olympic speed-skating team—
all men—poses in December 1923, just a few months
before the 1924 Winter Games.*

was still considered to be a man's sport. People would have been shocked to see a lady lift up her petticoats and race around the ice!

Speed skating became an official Olympic sport in 1924. But once again, only men were allowed to compete. Women were allowed to compete at the Olympics as figure skaters but not speed skaters.

When did the rules finally change? When were female speed skaters finally allowed to compete in the Olympics? Not until 1960—just four years before Bonnie Blair was born!

Twenty-four years later, Bonnie was on her way to the 1984 Olympics in Sarajevo. She was ready to do her best—as a representative of the United States, as a female athlete, and, most importantly, as a speed skater.

6

Off to the Olympics

Bonnie was a long shot for a gold medal in the 1984 Winter Olympics. She knew that even before she arrived in Sarajevo. The tall, strong East German speed skaters seemed unbeatable that year. But that didn't stop Bonnie from trying her hardest.

Sarajevo is a city in southeastern Europe. The airfare from Illinois was very expensive, so only Bonnie's mother and two of her sisters made the trip to watch Bonnie compete in her first Olympic games. The rest of her family had to watch on television back home.

Sarajevo was a picture of winter beauty on the day of Bonnie's race. Years later, a

Bonnie battles a heavy snowfall during the 500-meter women's speed-skating race at the Sarajevo 1984 Winter Olympics.

horrible civil war would turn this city into a bloody battleground. The Olympic skating rinks would be bombed out. The site of the opening ceremonies would be transformed into a graveyard. But on that day back in 1984, Sarajevo's lovely old bridges were covered in a peaceful blanket of snow. That's how Bonnie likes to remember it.

There was only one problem with all the snow. It completely buried the outdoor skating rink where Bonnie was supposed to race! Someone would have to clear the rink. But there wasn't a snowplow in sight.

Finally, some work crews appeared. Slowly, the men started clearing the rink with shovels. It took them so long that the start of the race had to be delayed for seven hours!

The wait was frustrating. But Bonnie didn't complain. The only thing to do was to "try and be cool about it," she told a reporter.

Patiently, Bonnie counted down the hours until her race. Her years of training had taught her an important lesson: a good athlete should always be a good sport. And good sports never lose their temper.

At last, it was time for Bonnie to hit the ice. She skated as fast as her legs could carry her on that cold, snowy day. But she couldn't keep up with the East German skaters. Bonnie finished in eighth place.

Was she discouraged? No. The 1984 Olympics only made Bonnie more determined to try again. Sarajevo was just the warm-up act. The real excitement was yet to come.

7

Gold!

Bonnie's next chance at an Olympic medal was four years away. But it was not too early to start planning. Bonnie arranged her life around her training. Her Olympic coach, Mike Crowe, lived in Butte, Montana. So in 1986, Bonnie moved to Butte, too.

Bonnie liked Montana, with its rugged mountains and wide-open plains. She lived with the family of another speed skater, Dave Silk. Bonnie and Dave had fun working out together. But as much as she enjoyed her new life in Butte, Bonnie was rarely there during the winter racing season.

That was because winter is *the* busy time for speed skaters. There are competitions all

Bonnie and her coach, Mike Crowe.

over the world. And by now, Bonnie had been traveling the globe for quite some time. In 1987 alone, she raced on thirteen different

Bonnie in 1987, at the age of twenty-three.

tracks throughout the world.

Bonnie quickly got used to living out of a suitcase. She didn't mind waking up in different countries. She didn't mind long plane flights.

But there was one thing Bonnie *did* mind about traveling. She missed watching afternoon soap operas on television. Watching TV had always been Bonnie's favorite way to relax after a hard workout. Now, she hated not knowing what was happening to her favorite soap-opera characters.

Bonnie's mother came up with a solution. Whenever Bonnie was out of the country for a long time, Mrs. Blair would send Bonnie detailed updates on the soap operas. That way Bonnie never lost touch with her favorite shows...or her family.

Bonnie was happy dedicating her life to speed skating. And it showed on the ice. She was skating so well that people started talking about her. Reporters started interviewing her. Articles started appearing. And the pressure started building as the 1988 Olympics approached.

Just a few weeks before the Olympics,

Bonnie's picture appeared on the cover of *Life* magazine. The caption read "Best Bet for U.S. Gold." It seemed as if the whole country was counting on Bonnie to win a gold medal. Could she do it?

As the 1988 Olympics drew near, Bonnie and her family received some upsetting news. Her father was told he had lung cancer. And just around the same time, Bonnie's brother Rob was told he had a brain tumor. The doctors said they couldn't operate on Rob's tumor.

Bonnie's family tried to keep their spirits up. They didn't want the illnesses to ruin Bonnie's chances at the Olympics. And Bonnie knew that her winning a gold medal would be the best medicine for both her brother and her father.

Mr. Blair and Rob were both well enough to make the trip to Calgary, Canada, for the 1988 Winter Olympics. But they weren't the only ones rooting for Bonnie. Her huge fan club in Calgary attracted just as much attention as Bonnie herself!

Reporters called Bonnie's crowd of family and friends the "Blair Bunch." You couldn't miss them in the grandstands. They all wore blue-and-white jackets with Bonnie's name on the front. They waved big banners and American flags. In loud voices, they sang Bonnie's theme song, "My Bonnie Lies Over the Ocean."

The Blair Bunch gave Bonnie strength. And all her determination and training paid off. It was in Calgary that Bonnie set the world record in the 500-meter race.

She dedicated her first gold medal to her brother Rob.

Bonnie's family couldn't believe that their little tagalong was now an Olympic gold medalist. They jokingly took turns biting her medal, just to make sure it was real gold.

Bonnie's large crowd of family and friends became known as the "Blair Bunch." They followed her to all her races and gave her tremendous support.

Bonnie celebrates her world-record gold-medal win in the 500-meter speed-skating event at the Olympic Winter Games in Calgary, Canada. She is surrounded by her brother Rob, her sister Suzy, and her nephew Scott Polaski.

Soon, the celebrating had to stop. Bonnie still had two more races ahead of her in Calgary. She had to get ready again, physically and mentally.

Bonnie managed a third-place finish in the 1,000-meter race a few days later. She now had a bronze medal to wear with the gold one.

But by the day of the 1,500-meter race, Bonnie was exhausted. She just couldn't seem to come up with the energy she needed. Bonnie didn't win a medal, but she came in fourth in this final race.

The disappointment didn't last long, however. The U.S. Olympic Committee gave Bonnie the honor of carrying the American flag at the closing ceremonies.

Bonnie was the only American athlete to win two medals at the 1988 Olympics. Never in her life had Bonnie been so proud of herself...or so proud to be an American.

8

Olympic Fame

Bonnie's skating skills had come to her naturally. Dealing with fame was a different story. Bonnie could be herself on the ice. But off the ice, she sometimes felt awkward being a celebrity.

Crowds of reporters wanted to interview Bonnie after the 1988 Olympics. She was surprised that some of these reporters knew very little about speed skating.

But Bonnie was always polite and patient with the news media. Even if a reporter didn't know the difference between pack racing and Olympic-style racing. Even if she was answering the same question for the tenth time that day!

Whenever Bonnie was interviewed, her answers were honest and to the point. She never pretended to be anything other than what she was...a girl from the Midwest who loved to skate fast.

Shortly after the Olympics, Bonnie received an invitation that made her heart race as fast as her skates. President Ronald

Bonnie meets with President Ronald Reagan at the White House shortly after the 1988 Winter Olympics. Behind the president is gold medal–winning figure skater Brian Boitano.

Reagan had invited her to the White House!

Bonnie was thrilled to be a guest of the president. But she was also a little nervous. What she would have liked was a peanut butter and jelly sandwich to calm her stomach. Instead, she found herself at an elegant White House dinner, looking around the room in disbelief.

After the dinner, Vice President George Bush came up to Bonnie. "I saw you kind of staring around the room during dinner," he said. "Sometimes I can't believe I'm here either." It was a nice thing for Mr. Bush to say. It helped make Bonnie feel more relaxed.

Back at home in Illinois, Bonnie felt more comfortable with her new role as a star. When the Chicago White Sox asked her to throw out the first pitch at a baseball game, she gladly accepted. And when the Chicago Cubs held a game in which celebrities played against old-timers, Bonnie was in true form.

Bonnie (center) cheers with her teammates during a 1988 Cubs game in which celebrities played against old-timers.

She made the game-saving catch in the final inning. Bonnie had always loved softball, and it showed!

Bonnie also enjoyed herself at a huge welcome-home reception thrown by the people of Champaign. A local jeweler made Bonnie a special diamond necklace. It had thirty-nine diamonds—one for each of the thirty-nine seconds it had taken Bonnie to skate the 500-meter race.

Bonnie's sister later joked that Bonnie was probably one of the only girls who would have been happier with one less diamond. That's because Bonnie's goal was to skate the 500-meter in thirty-eight seconds.

Bonnie was overwhelmed by fan mail in the weeks after the Olympics. One envelope had nothing on it except Bonnie's name and the words "Olympic Gold Medalist."

"No address, no stamp—and it got to my house," Bonnie said. She couldn't believe she was *that* famous.

Some of the fan mail made Bonnie laugh. "I wish to congratulate you on winning the Gold Medal," one third-grader wrote. "I was going to be there, but I had to go to my aunt's house. So I watched it on TV. It was a good show."

Finally, after a few months, the attention began to fade. Bonnie could get back to a normal life.

Bonnie decided to skate a little less and study a little more, so she took some college classes at Montana Tech. "Being competitive in sports," Bonnie said, "I found myself being competitive in school. I wanted to get a better grade."

Bonnie did just that. She became a winner in the classroom, earning A's in applied health and chemistry, and B's in computer science and economics.

But Bonnie wanted to remain a winner in sports, too, and so she started looking for new ways to challenge herself. One of those ways was with a new sport—cycling!

For four months, Bonnie ignored her skates. She even moved to Indianapolis to train as a cyclist. And even though she was new to the sport, Bonnie finished fourth in her very first national sprint competition!

Bonnie's speed-skating coach wasn't too happy. "He gets the feeling that cycling tends to take away from skating," Bonnie explained at the time. "He feels that cycling doesn't give much back."

Soon, Bonnie had to make a choice. Which would it be—speed skating or cycling? Bonnie enjoyed riding fast on her bicycle. But she could go even faster on the ice.

Bonnie knew she couldn't give up speed skating. After all, it was her life. So she put all her energy back into her favorite sport. But there were some disappointments ahead.

9

Difficult Times

It was Christmas Eve, 1989. Bonnie was doing what she liked to do best. She was out on the ice, skating as fast as she could.

Bonnie's father was doing what he liked to do best, too. He was watching Bonnie skate. But Charlie Blair wasn't feeling well. His long battle with lung cancer had weakened him. And now he had pneumonia. But seeing Bonnie skate filled Mr. Blair with happiness, pride, and love.

The next day, Charlie Blair died. It was a sad Christmas for the Blair family. Bonnie remembered how her father had always been there for her. She could picture him, stopwatch in hand, timing her races, pushing her to go faster, always believing in her.

Bonnie wanted to honor her father. She knew only one way to do that. She would continue to skate her best. And she would win races, in his memory.

Bonnie won many races that cold winter. There wasn't a single American speed skater who even came close to challenging her.

But Bonnie's luck did not last through the next racing season. She came down with a terrible case of bronchitis and had trouble breathing. And she had even more trouble skating.

Without her usual energy, Bonnie started losing races. She couldn't even get comfortable on her own skates. She'd often look down at her feet as if wondering whose skates she was wearing.

Nothing seemed to go right that season. Bonnie was racing in Europe when war broke out in the Persian Gulf. People were worried about the safety of the American speed skaters. Would someone try to attack them because they were from the United States?

Officials decided to end the racing season early. The American skaters were told to pack their bags and prepare to go home. Their travel plans were kept secret so they would not be in danger. It was a dramatic ending to a disappointing season.

Bonnie needed to get out of her slump. She finally decided a new coach might help, and she parted ways with Mike Crowe. Her new coach was Peter Mueller, a 1976 Olympic gold medalist.

Coach Mueller made Bonnie work hard during the hot, humid summer. Indoor rinks could get very crowded. So Bonnie often trained outdoors on in-line roller skates.

With time, Bonnie's confidence returned. And so did her strength and her speed. "She's back now skating the way she knows how to skate," Coach Mueller told a reporter at the end of 1991.

Bonnie had someone else helping her behind the scenes. His name was David Cruikshank. David was a twenty-two-year-old speed skater from Northbrook, Illinois. Bonnie and David shared a love for their sport. And when they started dating, they also shared a common goal. They both wanted to make the 1992 Olympic team.

Bonnie poses with David Cruikshank in her mother's home in July 1994.

David Cruikshank had failed to make the Olympic team in 1988. But he was eager to try again. So Bonnie and David trained together. They motivated each other to work harder.

At the Olympic tryouts in Wisconsin, Bonnie watched David nervously. Now she could understand how her parents had felt, watching her from the sidelines.

David didn't let her down. For the first time, he made the Olympic team. And for the third time, Bonnie qualified as well. Together, they would enjoy the thrill of representing the United States in Albertville, France, the site of the 1992 Winter Games.

10

Double Gold!

Bonnie Blair had a chance to make history in the 1992 Winter Olympics in Albertville. All she had to do was win another gold medal. No American woman had ever won back-to-back gold medals at two Winter Olympics. Would Bonnie be the first?

Victory was not certain. A Chinese skater named Ye Qiaobo (YAY CHAH-boh) wanted desperately to beat Bonnie. To prepare for the race, Ye had studied videotapes of Bonnie skating. Ye was determined to learn the secrets of Bonnie's speed. And she was determined to win.

Bonnie was looking forward to a hard race against Ye Qiaobo. But first, she had some important business to take care of. It was so important that Bonnie even missed the opening ceremonies of the 1992 Winter Olympics.

Bonnie had to do her laundry! And she figured this would be a perfect time. Laundry was not Bonnie's idea of fun. But neither was waiting in line for a washing machine.

There were only five washing machines in the entire Olympic Village, which was where hundreds of athletes stayed. And Bonnie figured that no one else would be doing their laundry during the opening ceremonies. Bonnie waited until all the athletes had gone to the ceremonies before lugging her dirty clothes to the machines.

The Olympic Village in Albertville had some other problems. Bonnie's room was a long walk from the restaurant where the athletes ate. And the skating rink was even farther away. Bonnie had to spend one and a half hours on a bus traveling to and from the rink. To make matters worse, the rink was outdoors, which meant that the ice was often slushy.

Conditions were not perfect in Albertville. But Bonnie tried not to complain. She wasn't just a good athlete. She was a good sport. And her cheering section this year was bigger than ever.

More than forty of Bonnie's relatives and friends came to Albertville. The ever-growing Blair Bunch ranged in age from Bonnie's four-month-old nephew to her eighty-year-old Uncle Lenny. And even Bonnie's brother Rob managed to get there. No one wanted to miss out on the fun.

The Blair Bunch had a new outfit made up for Albertville. They all wore purple-and-white windbreakers, with Bonnie's name on the front and back. Section 19 in the grand-stands was Blair territory. You could see it. And you could *hear* it.

You couldn't miss the Blair Bunch at the 1992 Olympics in Albertville, France. A whole section of the grandstands was set aside for them.

Bonnie's fans were ready for her race against Ye Qiaobo. But they were unusually quiet as Bonnie did her warm-up laps. Bonnie had told them she wanted to concentrate. So they kept their mouths shut, just as she had asked. For the Blair Bunch, that was a major accomplishment!

Ye Qiaobo skated before Bonnie. The ice was wet that day. But Ye still managed to skate 500 meters in only 40.51 seconds. That meant Ye was in first place when Bonnie took to the ice.

Bonnie had spent years training for this moment. Yet the race would be over in less than a minute. That is one of the hardest things about being a professional speed skater.

Bonnie crouched into her starting position. She thought of her father. Then, as the starting gun went off, all thoughts disappeared. Her instincts took over. Bonnie Blair raced as fast as she could, heading for the finish line.

The clock stopped at 40.33 seconds. But Bonnie's heart continued pounding hard. She had done it! By just eighteen hundredths of a second, Bonnie had beaten Ye Qiaobo.

Bonnie pulled off the hood of her red, white, and blue racing skin. She shook her brunette hair and raised her arms toward the stands.

David Cruikshank was bursting with pride. Bonnie's mother breathed a sigh of relief. "I'm shaking all over," Mrs. Blair told a reporter. "I guess I held my breath too long. I don't think I took one breath during that whole race."

But there were more nervous moments ahead. Eleven pairs of skaters still had to race. The crowd watched and waited. But no one managed to top Bonnie's time.

Bonnie Blair was now a two-time gold medal winner. She dedicated her second gold medal to her father's memory. Bonnie wished he were still alive. But she knew he was there in spirit, cheering her on to victory.

Bonnie's second race, two days later, was a disappointment. For this competition, skaters had to race 1,500 meters. Bonnie ran out of energy, and she came in twenty-first place.

That left Bonnie with one last chance at another medal—the 1,000-meter race. That

By just eighteen hundredths of a second, Bonnie beat Ye Qiaobo in the 500-meter speed-skating race in Albertville and won her second gold medal.

race was also Ye Qiaobo's last chance to beat Bonnie Blair in Albertville.

This time, Bonnie skated before Ye. The clock read 1:20.90 when Bonnie crossed the

Bonnie waves to the crowd after being awarded the Olympic gold medal for the 500-meter race in Albertville.

Bonnie is interviewed by a reporter after receiving the gold medal for the 1,000-meter race in Albertville. Looking on is her proud mother, Eleanor.

finish line. No one knew if Ye would skate faster. So there was no wild cheering at the end of this race. Bonnie waved briefly to the crowd and sat down on the bench.

The air was thick with tension when Ye approached the starting line. She pushed herself and pushed herself—to the limit. But Ye was two hundredths of a second slower than Bonnie.

Bonnie carries the American flag during the closing ceremonies of the 1992 Winter Olympics in Albertville, France.

It's hard to imagine two hundredths of a second making such a difference. But that tiny fraction of a second meant another gold medal for Bonnie Blair.

Bonnie was more relieved than excited. She had lots of hugs for her family and for David, who finished in twenty-second place in his race. But Bonnie did not dedicate her third gold medal to anyone in the Blair Bunch.

"This one," Bonnie said, "is just for winning."

11

A Golden Finish

Bonnie was lucky. She didn't have to wait another four years to compete again in the Olympics. Because of a change in the rules, the next Winter Olympics was scheduled for 1994—just two years away.

Bonnie knew she could not skate forever. She would be almost thirty years old by the winter of 1994. And that is fairly old for a speed skater.

Bonnie made a difficult decision. She decided that the 1994 Winter Olympics, which would take place in Norway, would be her fourth—and final—Olympics. After 1994, she would stop competing in the Olympics.

The two years passed quickly. Bonnie and David continued to work out together whenever they could.

David never seemed jealous of the attention Bonnie received. She was the Olympic superstar. He was simply a dedicated member of the Olympic team. That was how he saw it.

Bonnie was often gone for weeks at a time, racing overseas. Some of these long trips became a blur of skating and sleeping. But there was one night in February 1993 that Bonnie will never forget.

After the success of the 1992 Winter Olympics, Bonnie was often gone for weeks at a time, racing overseas. Here she receives a medal in Ikaho, Japan, after racing in the two-day World Sprint Skating Championships.

She was training in Germany for the World Cup finals. She'd gone to bed early so she'd have the strength for her workout the next day. At 3:45 A.M., Bonnie was jolted out of her sleep by a telephone call. It was her mother, calling long-distance from Illinois with great news.

"You won the Sullivan Award!" Mrs. Blair said. It took a few seconds for the news to sink in. The Sullivan Award is one of the highest honors an amateur athlete can receive. The list of past winners includes speed skater Eric Heiden and basketball legend Bill Bradley.

Bonnie was the first Sullivan Award winner in fourteen years to miss the presentation. After all, she really hadn't expected to win. The list of nine other nominees that year had included the popular figure skater Kristi Yamaguchi. But the judges chose Bonnie. What a way to start the day!

The Sullivan Award helped motivate Bonnie between Olympics. So did another coaching switch. Bonnie's new coach, Nick Thometz, changed her training schedule. Now she worked out for four days, then rested for one day.

"She's been doing the same thing for so long that motivation can be a problem," Thometz told a reporter. "I've tried some different things with her. I think it's been a plus."

Motivation was definitely not a problem for Bonnie's cheerleading section. Their problem was money. Everyone in the Blair Bunch wanted to be in Norway for Bonnie's final Olympic race. But the airfare and lodgings were very expensive.

People in the village of Hammar, Norway, came up with a solution. They had admired the fun-loving Blair Bunch at earlier Olympics. So they offered lodging in their homes to Bonnie's family, for very little cost.

The people of Hammar were happy to help out. And they were proud of Viking Hall, their town's new indoor skating rink, where Bonnie would make her Olympic farewell.

Viking Hall was a speed skater's dream, and Bonnie couldn't wait to get on the ice.

Reporters knew Bonnie Blair could make big news in Norway. If she could win two more gold medals, she would have more golds than any other American female athlete!

But as it turned out, Bonnie was not the center of attention at the 1994 Olympics. Newspeople spent much more time covering the story of two American figure skaters—Nancy Kerrigan and Tonya Harding.

Several weeks before the Olympics began, someone snuck into a rink in Detroit, Michigan, where Nancy Kerrigan was practicing.

Bonnie takes her laps during the workout session in Lillehammer, Norway.

This person hit her in the legs with a metal bar. It was obvious that the person was trying to prevent her from competing. Tonya Harding was suspected of helping plan the surprise attack. In the weeks that followed, the American public wanted to know everything about their rivalry.

Compared with the battle between the two figure skaters, the Bonnie Blair story was sweet and simple. Here was someone who loved to skate, who worked hard to win, and

Bonnie and her fellow teammates wave to the crowd during the Opening Ceremonies for the 1994 Winter Olympics in Lillehammer, Norway.

who enjoyed sharing her success with her family and friends. Her loving family was firmly behind her. And her steady boyfriend was one of her biggest supporters. There was nothing flashy about Bonnie Blair...except when she was speeding toward the finish line!

Bonnie's Olympic career came to a golden end in Norway. First, she won the gold medal in her favorite race, the 500-meter. In the 1,500-meter race, which had given her trouble before, Bonnie skated the fastest she ever had. She didn't win a medal in that race. But she was happy anyway, for she knew she had skated her personal best.

Then came Bonnie's final race, the 1,000-meter. This was her final chance to win a record-breaking fifth gold medal. The pressure was on. And Bonnie could feel it. But it only made her go faster. She won the race by 1.38 seconds. That's a *big* chunk of time in speed skating.

Once again, Bonnie Blair had made Olympic history. One reporter in Norway called her "America's shining star." In Bonnie's final Olympic news conference, another reporter tried to pinpoint the secret of her success. Was it fear of not being the best?

Bonnie celebrates her victory after winning the 500-meter race in Lillehammer, Norway.

After the 1,000-meter race in Lillehammer, Norway, Bonnie flashes five fingers to represent her fifth Olympic gold medal.

Bonnie looked at the reporter as if he were crazy. "I don't fear anything," she said simply. No one doubted her for a second.

12

Skating Away

A Winter Olympics without Bonnie Blair will be like a peanut butter sandwich without the jelly. Something sweet will be missing!

Through four Winter Games, Americans have come to love Bonnie's smile and her good sportsmanship. Her constant victories have been a source of pride. And without the wild Blair Bunch, the grandstands will seem very quiet.

Bonnie says she may return to the Olympics, just for the fun of watching other athletes compete. She may also become a coach. Who knows? Maybe with Bonnie's help, more American speed skaters will strike gold.

*Bonnie skates with New York City schoolchildren at
Central Park's Wollman Rink.*

But will there ever be a speed skater as
fast as Bonnie Blair? So far, there's only one
American speed skater who has been able to
break Bonnie's record times. And that's Bonnie Blair herself!

A month after the Olympics in Norway, Bonnie broke her own record in the 500-meter. All her life, she had dreamed of skating that race in less than thirty-nine seconds. When she finally did, at a sprint meet in Calgary, Bonnie waited for the thunderous applause.

She waited. And waited. Then she remembered. This was not the Winter Olympics. There were fewer than a hundred people in the grandstands. No wonder the applause wasn't deafening! Even so, Bonnie was satisfied. She had shattered the thirty-nine-second barrier. Now she could even remove one of the thirty-nine diamonds from her necklace!

A year later, Bonnie did it again. She was back in Calgary, on her farewell tour. In one month, she would hang up her skates for good. In one month, she would turn thirty-one.

The final Calgary races did not start off

well for Bonnie. She lost a 500-meter race to a Canadian woman, Susan Auch. Bonnie's fans were worried. Had she finally run out of energy?

Bonnie's coach wasn't worried. "She's not inhuman," Nick Thometz said. "She doesn't go out and feel like a gold medalist every day. She has bad days. But some people will say, 'Oh, I don't feel good today,' and write it off. If Bonnie's day isn't good, she'll try to work through it, and she'll try to make it better."

Thometz was right. The next day, Bonnie had to compete in another 500-meter race against Auch. Now Bonnie was more determined than ever. She overtook Auch in the first 100 meters. Then she sped toward a new world record of 38.69 seconds.

Today, Bonnie is striving to fulfill other dreams. She hopes to finish college, marry, and start a

Bonnie displays one of her medals to a group of schoolchildren in New York City.

family. Given her history, her children may learn to skate even before they can walk!

Bonnie will have many wonderful stories to pass on to her children and grandchildren. Stories of breathtaking finishes. Stories of faraway countries where she has raced. Stories of Olympic gold.

Bonnie also has an awesome collection of awards and trophies. But she makes one thing very clear. She didn't work hard at her sport just to collect gold medals.

"I don't think winning means anything in particular," Bonnie once said. "It's the satisfaction you get from knowing you did your best."

WENDY DALY worked for eleven years as a television newswriter in Boston, Massachusetts. She learned all about skating and cold Midwestern winters when she and her family moved briefly to Bonnie Blair's home state of Illinois. Ms. Daly now lives with her husband and three children in Barrington, Rhode Island. This is her first book for children.

Other Bullseye Biographies You'll Enjoy: